SUGAR GROVE PUBLIC LIBRARY DISTRICT
54 Snow Street/P.O. Box 1049
Sugar Grove, IL 60554
(630) 466-4686

5/31/05

www.sugargrove.lib.il.us

SUGAR GROVE PUBLIC LIBRARY DISTRICT
54 Snow St. / 466-4686
Hours: Mon. - Thurs. 10 am - 9 pm
Hours: Fri. & Sat. 10 am - 5 pm

For David—because it's your story!
—R. H. H.

THANK YOU!
Thanks to all of you for sharing your expertise about young children:
Sarah Birss, M.D., child analyst and pediatrician, Cambridge, MA
Deborah Chamberlain, research associate, Norwood, MA
Ben Harris, elementary school teacher, New York, NY
Bill Harris, parent, Cambridge, MA
David Harris, pre-kindergarten/kindergarten teacher, New York, NY
Robyn Heilbrun, parent, Salt Lake City, UT
Ellen Kelley, director, The Cambridge-Ellis School, Cambridge, MA
Elizabeth A. Levy, children's book author, New York, NY
Janet Patterson, pre-kindergarten teacher, Shady Hill School, Cambridge, MA
Karen Shorr, pre-kindergarten teacher, The Brookwood School, Manchester, MA

First Aladdin Paperbacks edition November 2004

Text copyright © 2001 by Bee Productions, Inc.
Illustrations copyright © 2001 by Jan Ormerod

ALADDIN PAPERBACKS
An imprint of Simon & Schuster
Children's Publishing Division
1230 Avenue of the Americas
New York, NY 10020

Also available in a Margaret K. McElderry hardcover edition.
The text of this book was set in Bembo.
The illustrations are rendered in black pencil line and watercolor washes.

Manufactured in China
10 9 8 7 6 5 4 3 2 1

The Library of Congress has cataloged the hardcover edition as follows:
Haris, Robie H. Goodbye Mousie / by Robie H. Harris ; illustrated by Jan Ormerod.—1st ed.
p. cm.
Summary: A boy grieves for his dead pet Mousie, helps to bury him, and begins to come to
terms with his loss.
ISBN 0-689-83217-6 (hc.) [1. Death—Fiction. 2. Grief—Fiction. 3. Mice—Fiction. 4.
Pets—Fiction.]
I. Ormerod, Jan, ill. II. Title. PZ7.H2436 Go 2001 [E]—dc21 99-089167

ISBN 0-689-87134-1 (Aladdin pbk.)

Goodbye Mousie

by Robie H. Harris
illustrated by Jan Ormerod

ALADDIN PAPERBACKS
New York   London   Toronto   Sydney

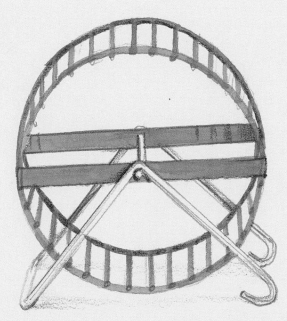

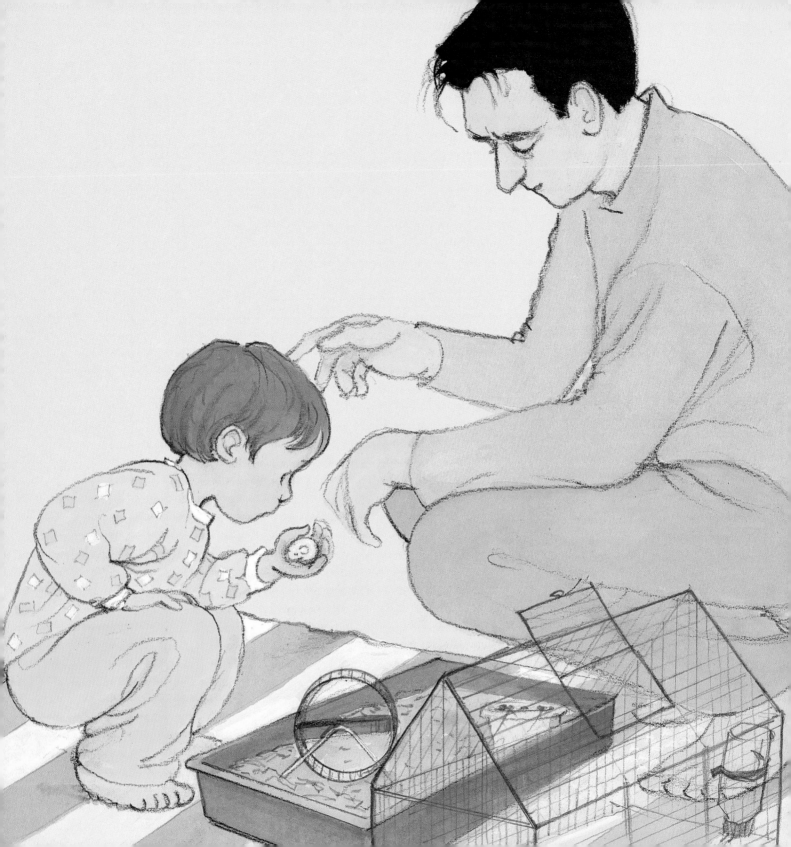

When I woke up this morning, I tickled Mousie's tummy. But Mousie didn't wake up. I tickled Mousie's chin, but he still didn't wake up. Then Daddy came to say good morning.

"Mousie won't wake up!" I whispered. "I think something's wrong!"

Daddy took a good look at Mousie. Then he put his arm around me.

"I have something very sad to tell you," he said. "Mousie is . . . dead."

And then Daddy gave me a big hug.

"It's NOT true!" I said. "Mousie's just sleeping. He'll wake up soon. He's just tired. You're wrong! Mousie did NOT die! Mousie is NOT dead!"

Daddy sat down on my bed and I put Mousie in his hand.

"I'm so sorry about Mousie," he said.

"Mousie is NOT dead!" I said again. "Mousie was alive last night! He's just . . . very . . . very sleepy this morning."

"Dead," said Daddy, "is very different from sleeping. Dead is—"

"—NOT alive!" I shouted. And I started to cry.

"You must be sad," said Daddy.

"I'm not sad. I'm mad! I'm mad at Mousie. I'm mad he died!"

And then I cried. I really cried.

Then I said, "I'm sad."

"I'm sad, too," said Daddy. And he gave me another hug.

"I want to hold Mousie again," I said. "I want to hold Mousie now."

"Okay," said Daddy.

I held Mousie again, but he felt cold. So I wrapped an old T-shirt around him.

"I don't like Mousie dead!" I said. "Why'd he die?"

"I don't think Mousie got hurt," said Daddy.
"But maybe he got too sick."

"Is that why he died?" I asked.

"Well," said Daddy, "Mousie was a baby when
we got him. He grew up. Then he grew old.
Mousie was very, very old for a mouse."

"So is that why he died?" I asked.

"I don't know if we'll ever know exactly why
Mousie died," said Daddy. "But Mousie did
have a good life."

"What'll we do with him now that he's . . . dead?"
I asked.

"We can bury him in the yard so he'll be close by,"
said Daddy.

"But how will I know exactly where he is?"

"We could make a sign."

"Can it say, MOUSIE IS RIGHT HERE?"

"Sure!" said Daddy. And he wrote MOUSIE IS RIGHT
HERE! in big letters on an old wooden board we'd
found at the beach.

I carried Mousie into the kitchen. Mommy gave me a hug and a kiss.

Then she gave me an extra hug and a kiss.

"I'm so sorry Mousie died," she said. And she handed me a shoebox.

"We could bury Mousie in this," she said. "Mousie will be safe in this."

I laid Mousie in the shoebox and tucked my old T-shirt all around him. Mommy made toast with strawberry jam on it for me. But I wasn't hungry at all.

"Do you think it's okay to bury Mousie with some toast?" I asked. "I always used to feed Mousie bites of my toast. Mousie loved toast."

"I think that would be just fine," said Mommy.

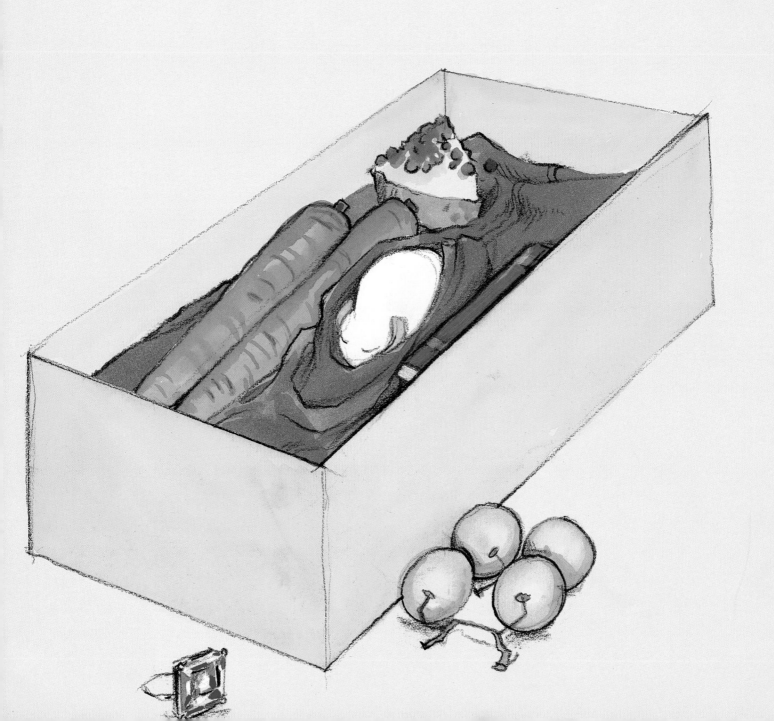

"Can I put more things in the box?" I asked.

"Of course you can!" said Mommy.

I put some toast and two whole carrots on one side of Mousie. I put four grapes and a chocolate candy bar on the other side.

"Now Mousie won't be hungry!" I said.

I put my red racing car in the box. I put a ring with a big blue jewel my dentist gave me in the box. I put an orange crayon in, too.

"Now Mousie won't be bored!" I said.

I taped a picture of me in sunglasses to the inside of the shoebox.

"Now Mousie won't be lonely," I said.

Then I taped the box shut and looked at it. "Mousie's box looks too plain," I said. "And Mousie won't like that."

So I painted wiggly stripes all over Mousie's box. I felt a little bit better. And Mousie's box didn't look plain anymore.

"It looks nice," said Daddy.

I thought it looked nice, too.

I washed almost all the paint off my hands. And now
I was hungry. So I went to take a bite of my toast.
But it was all gone!

"My toast!" I shouted. "Where'd it go? Did it die, too?"

"Oh no, sweetheart!" said Mommy. "I ate it. I thought
you weren't hungry. I'm really sorry. I'll toast another
piece for you."

"I don't want one. And I hate all this dying stuff!"
I cried. "Let's bury Mousie NOW!"

So we did.

Mommy dug a hole in the dirt and I put the shoebox in the hole.

Daddy stuck the sign in the dirt and I covered up the box with the dirt.

Mommy lit two sparklers and I stuck them in the dirt. We all watched the sparklers burn out. And I cried.

And then I said, "Mousie, I'm mad at you for being dead. I'm sad, too. You were a good mouse. I'll miss you, Mousie."

Then I cried some more and said, "Goodbye Mousie." That's all I said.

When I wake up tomorrow morning, Mousie won't be here. It's true. Mousie is dead.

I wish he would come back. But I don't think he will.
So, maybe someday, I'll get another mouse. But not just yet.